Uncommon Scents

Written and Illustrated by Elaine Beem Robinson

The story of Marvin the Muskrat and his peaceful triumph over bullies

Everfield Press

ISBN 978-1-946785-06-0

Dedicated to those who make peace everywhere

Of all the animals in the forest,
Marvin Muskrat was the poorest.

His family tree was limp as phlox is,
Not strong and sturdy like the ox's,

Or full of noble familious scions,
Like the lineage of lions,

Or laden with glorifying squawk,
As the family tree of hawk,

Or filled with beauty as resplendent,
As the peacock and descendent.

All with lineage grand and glorious,
Every critter in the foriest,

Every critter that he knew,
But not our humble Marvin, too.
You see, every creature in this theme
Had a cause for self-esteem,

Save Marvin, as we know,
For he was several rungs below

The other animals in the forest.
Marvin was indeed the poorest.

That wasn't Marvin's only curse.
There were several problems worse.
He had no job to make him proud,
Like the lions and that crowd.

His brain was small and none too keen,
Not swift nor slow, just in between.

He had no special social prowess,
As did the bull with all his cowess,

Nor lightning speed nor athletic grace,
Nor lilting voice nor aesthetic face,
Nor height nor weight nor none of that,

Just an ordinary rat.

In the daytime Marvin swam
In the lake beneath the dam,
Just chewing roots and slinging mud,
To build his home beside the wood.

And every afternoon at five,
All the animals alive
Came from forest far and near--
The foxes, otters, bears, and deer.
They played, they sang, they drank like fish;
They satisfied their smallest wish.
And every night at least one hoof,
Would cave in Marvin's well-made roof.

So, all the next day Marvin would
Chew more roots and sling more mud,
To patch his home the best he could,
On the lakeside near the wood.
All these creatures, smooth and wooly,

Every single one a **bully**.

And night after night, this beastly cult
Played out this scene with the same result.
And Marvin couldn't help but see
That everyone was more important than he.
When he pleaded them for mercy,
It made the situation worse. See,

Then they knew they'd got his goat,
So they'd gather round and gloat,
Kicking sand in Marvin's face,
Generally tearing up the place.

And what could little Marvin do
To stifle such a motley crew?

Because, as we know from our chorus,
Marvin Muskrat was the poorest
Of all the animals in the forest.

And no matter how high you set your sights,
As long as you're poor you have no rights.
You have no right to stand your ground,
To speak your piece or make a sound,
Or try to somehow slow the pace
Of critters who invade your space.
You have no option but to take it,
And if you're not happy, then you fake it,

While some beast of wit and wile
Makes mincemeat of your domicile.

Yet, Marvin admired their vigor and vim,
Since it wasn't much fun just being him.
And if Mother Nature said the word,
He'd trade in his Muskrat Union card
For any beastly occupation
Of any species, any nation,
Any occupation that
Elevated him from rat.

For he'd known since he was a pup,
From Muskrat, all directions are up.

Then one afternoon at five,
When all the animals alive
Were gallivanting all around,
From the woods there came a sound,
Like someone stamping on the ground.
And within seconds, such a rush
Of crashing branch and broken bush,
When legged beast or winged thrush,
Burst from the forest with a flush.

A stamp, a flush, and then a sigh,
It suddenly became so quiet.

"What wath that?" Marvin asked in wonder,
"To foment thuch a beathtly thunder?"
(Not only was he short in successes
He also had trouble with his *Esses*)
"A macho man with gun or tank?
An armed platoon of file and rank?
An elephant with aching tooth?
A wild tiger on the looth?"

Some loathsome beast beyond description
Must have stirred up such conniption.
Then from the forest there appeared
The loathsome beast the others feared,
So small and black and rather fat.
Just an ordinary *cat*.
Just a cat, as slow as snails,
Decked out fine, in tux and tails.

Leastways, that's what Marvin thunk.
Truth was, though, it was a skunk.

And Marvin Muskrat was so poor
He'd never seen a skunk before.

But all the others had, so they
Kicked up their heels and ran away.

"How do," the small skunk paused to say,
"It seems I've chased your guests away.
I'd like to stay and chat, but first
I need a drink to quench my thirst."
(A polite, if loathsome, beast was that)
Thought Marvin, of the scary cat.
And when the skunk had drunk his fill,
He waddled up to Marvin's hill,
Plopped right down on Marvin's mound,
Eating grubs picked off the ground.

Marvin marveled at the fact
That this small cat, with deft and tact,
Had set the tyrants on the run,
Without the need of fang or gun.
Such a stupefying task!
And so, he drummed up nerve to ask,
"How'd you manage that effect?
What'd you do to earn rethpect?"

"They run away from me, I think.
For the simple reason that I stink."

"You thtink?"

"I do"

"Not now."

"That's true. But when I'm goaded to my limit
By some featherheaded dimwit,
And have no chance to get away,
I turn my back on them and spray.
But since everyone around here knew it,
I had no opportunity to do it."

That'th thum talent," Marvin said
(He wished he were a skunk instead!)

"I have no talent thuch ath that
I'm jutht a plain and thimple rat."

"You don't seem plain at all to me,
If you built this home from mud and tree,"
The skunk remarked perceptively.
"An extraordinary occupation!
While I've just built a reputation."

Now Marvin rubbed his furry head,
Pondering what the skunk just said.

But what he built up the others tore down,
He thought to himself with a frown.
"I haven't a thing," he admitted aloud,
"That ith the equal of all of that crowd.
I haven't their courage, their vigor or vim."

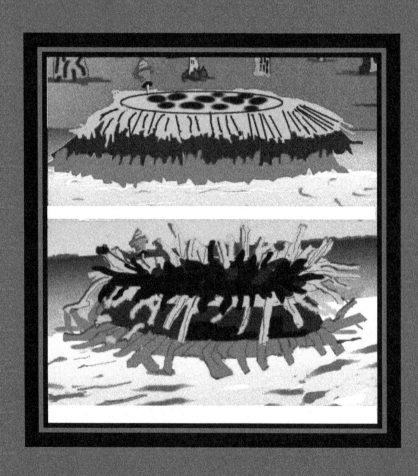

The skunk munched a grub and replied,
"You can swim.
So if I were in your place and the animals tried
To tear up my home, I would not run and hide.
I'd puff up my chest, never quiver nor quake,
Then I'd move all my stuff to the midst of the lake,

With a watery moat that is deep and immense,
Which will provide you an upperclass line of defense.
(Course I'm just a skunk, but I'm loaded with sense.)"

"But ithn't that chicken?" Marvin asked him.

"'Course not," the skunk replied,
"Chickens don't swim."

"It's just common sense to do
What you do best.
Tho' sense isn't as common
As you might have guessed."

The skunk munched a grub then he waddled away,
He had several meetings to go to that day.
But he left Marvin richer at least by one friend, and
He wished Marvin luck as he rounded the bend,
Although luck wouldn't help Marvin out in the end.

Marv needed instinct and Marv needed the skill,
To engineer sticks and mud into a hill.
He could do it himself with the know-how to make
A building from scratch in the midst of a lake.
Not everyone else can do marvelous things
From some mud and some roots
And some weeds and some strings.
After all, common sense isn't skunk-kind's alone,
For muskrats are noted for scents of their own.

And what Marvin did best was so easy for him.
It was easy to plan, and to build, and to swim.
Such that Marvin the Muskrat, the meek and demur,
Never once gave a thought to what talents *these* were!

So back to the mud and the roots in the lake,
Back to the work that makes backsliders shake,
Back to the dirt and the labor and sweat,
Back to the backache, the blister and wet.

With the critters around, getting into the way,

Wondering what Marvin Muskrat
Was up to that day.

He butterflied past them,
Avoiding their jeers.

He slipped 'neath the stomachs,
And slapped past their rears.

They could laugh all they wanted.
Whatever they'd say

Didn't matter to Marvin,
As he backstroked away.

He built him a new home and built it up right.

Then he packed his belongings, he labored all night.

But this time he avoided his early mistake,
And he built his home right in the midst of the lake,
Where the water is deeper than ever before,
When he lived on the mound
That was next to the shore.

So then, when the animals were so compelled
To tease and be hateful and not be dispelled,
In order to do so, they'd have to get wet,
And they'd have to be swimmers, and it's a safe bet

That Marvin could swim rings around all those that tried.
And just knowing he could made him happy inside.

Besides a new home with a 360 view
Of the water and weasels and wapitis too,
In the end of the day, Marvin triumphed in more
Than just building a nest far away from the shore.
He didn't triumph in riches or wealth or in size,
Or in beauty or bounty or in being so wise.

He wasn't a lion, he never would be,
Nor the leaf off a privileged family tree.
He was just a small muskrat, yet a rat who could swim,
Traverse dreadful creatures with valor and vim,
In the blink of an eye or just on a whim,

And with relative ease,
No mortgage nor lease,
Build a waterfront home, so tidy and trim,
That all of the animals marvel at *him*!

The End

Author and Illustrator Elaine Beem Robinson lives in Gainesville, Florida, along with husband, Ron, Snuffy the Schnauzer, and several retired racehorses, who reside in the backyard.

Having spent many years at the University of Florida as a research microbiologist, she contributed some to the plethora of articles written on the misdeeds of bacteria. Yet, she noted little on record about the virtuous muskrat. This poem is a tribute to muskrats and peace builders everywhere.